Tales of
Little Grey Rabbit

Alison Uttley was born in Derbyshire and at first educated at a tiny village school. She went to Manchester University, graduating in physics, and then spent a year at Cambridge where she transferred her enthusiasm from science to literature.

When her husband died, leaving her with a little son, she began to write books on country life and animals, incorporating in them many of the tales she had already told to children. The first *Little Grey Rabbit* stories were written in the 1930s and they are now well-known worldwide.

Alison Uttley was a gifted storyteller with admirers all over the world. She died in 1976 at the age of ninety-one.

D0047996

Also by Alison Uttley
in Piccolo

The Brown Mouse Book

Alison Uttley

Tales of
Little Grey Rabbit

Illustrated by Faith Jaques

Piccolo Books
in association with Heinemann

This collection first published 1980 by William Heinemann Ltd
This Piccolo edition published 1982 by Pan Books Ltd,
Cavaye Place, London SW10 9PG
in association with William Heinemann Ltd
The tales were first published in 1929, 1930, 1931, 1932
This collection © J. C. T. Uttley 1980
Illustrations © Faith Jaques 1980, 1982
ISBN 0 330 26601 2

Photoset by Parker Typesetting Service, Leicester
Printed and bound in England by
Richard Clay (The Chaucer Press) Ltd, Bungay, Suffolk

Contents

The Squirrel, the Hare, and the Little Grey Rabbit

A long time ago there lived in a little house on the edge of a wood, a Hare, a Squirrel, and a little Grey Rabbit.

The Hare, who wore a blue coat on weekdays and a red coat on Sundays, was a conceited fellow.

The Squirrel, who wore a brown dress on weekdays, and a yellow dress on Sundays, was proud.

But the little Rabbit, who always wore a grey dress with white collar and cuffs, was not proud at all.

Every morning when the birds began to twitter she sprang out of her bed in the attic and ran downstairs to the kitchen. She went into the shed for firewood, and lighted the fire. Then she filled her kettle with clear water from the brook which ran past the door, just beyond the garden.

While the water boiled she swept the floor and dusted the kitchen. She put the three small chairs round the table and spread a blue and white cloth. She made the tea in a brown teapot from daisy-heads which she kept in a canister on the dresser, and then she called the Squirrel and the Hare.

'Squirrel, wake up! Hare, Hare, breakfast is ready.'

Downstairs they strolled, rubbing their eyes, and wriggling their ears, but the little Grey Rabbit was already in the garden, gathering lettuce.

She placed one bunch in front of the Hare, one in front of the Squirrel, and a very small bunch on her own plate. In the middle of the table she put a bowl of nuts, and beside it a jam-pot full of honeysuckle.

'Good morning, Grey Rabbit,' yawned the Hare. 'I declare you have given us lettuce again. Really, my dear, you must think of something new for breakfast.'

'Good morning, Grey Rabbit,' said the Squirrel. 'Where's the milk? You know I cannot begin the day without a drink of milk.'

The little Grey Rabbit hung her head.

'It hasn't come yet,' she said.

'Tut, tut,' exclaimed the Squirrel. 'Late again. We must get another milkman.' But she knew she couldn't for there was only one who could milk the cows.

Just then 'Tap, tap, tap', sounded on the door. Little Grey Rabbit ran to open it and there stood the Hedgehog with a pint of milk.

'I nearly didn't get here at all,' said he. 'Such a dreadful thing has happened! A Weasel has come to live in the wood, in one of those tumble-down houses where nobody lives. They say it isn't safe to be out after dusk, for he prowls about in the dark, and you don't know what might happen. They say he goes hunting, and they say—' Here the Hedgehog whispered something.

The little Grey Rabbit shivered and looked all round her, at the lavender bushes and the dande-lion bed, as if the Weasel might be there.

'Only this morning, as I was milking the cow in the Farmer's field,' continued the Hedgehog breathlessly, 'I saw a dark figure glide over a wall, and I knew it was he. I had to lie still in the long grass and pretend I was a stone until the road was clear again. That's why I am so late.'

'Oh dear!' murmured the Grey Rabbit, 'I am

so glad you were not hurt, Mr Hedgehog. You must take care of yourself, even if we *do* go without milk.'

'Bless your heart, my pretty dear,' he smiled. 'You shall have your milk as long as old Hedgehog has some prickles left.'

'Well, good day,' he continued, 'and take care of yourself, and warn those two grumblers within there,' and off he hobbled.

'Whatever have you been talking about all this time?' asked the Squirrel angrily.

'Why was the milkman so late?' demanded the Hare.

Little Grey Rabbit drew her chair close up to them. 'He says a Weasel has come to live in the wood nearby, and it frightened him.'

'A Weasel, child?' said the Hare. 'Pooh! Who's afraid of a Weasel? A Weasel could never catch me! Shut the kitchen door, and pull the bolt. A draught might get in,' and he looked behind him nervously.

'You mean a Weasel,' exclaimed the Squirrel. 'Not that I mind any Weasel. I can climb, and I should like to see anyone follow me up a tree!'

But she shut the window and poked the fire, and kept the poker in her hand whilst she drank her milk.

'Tap, tap, tap' came on the door.

'Who's that?' asked the Squirrel anxiously.

'Go to the door, Grey Rabbit, and only open it a

crack,' said the Hare, running to the foot of the stairs.

Grey Rabbit opened the door a crack.

'It's only Robin Redbreast with the letters,' cried she. 'Come in, Robin, you quite startled us.'

A gay little bird hopped into the room, and put the letters on the table.

'One for Squirrel and one for Hare, and none for Grey Rabbit,' said he, with his head on one side, looking at them.

'Have you heard the news?' they asked.

'Oh, about the Weasel? Yes, I saw him this morning, early. He's a great big fellow with very sharp teeth. *I* shouldn't like to meet him on a dark night. We are putting barbed thorns round our nest, and there is a guard at the post office. 'Well, I must be off, I am busy today, I have to warn the birds,' and away he flew.

All day the Hare and the Squirrel stayed in the kitchen. The little Grey Rabbit ran upstairs and made the beds. She swept the floors, dusted and tidied up after the other two. Then she got her basket and started out to do the marketing.

'You might get me a new teasel brush,' called the Squirrel. 'I must give my tail a good brush, it is quite tangled.'

'And get me some young carrots,' shouted the Hare. 'I am tired of lettuce for breakfast.'

Off ran the little Grey Rabbit, in her clean white collar and cuffs, and her basket on her arm. Over the brook she leapt, and then she went into the wood. She kept a very sharp lookout, and ran so softly that the leaves underfoot scarcely moved, and the grass hardly felt her weight. Once she heard a rustle behind her, but she went steadily on and dared not turn her head. Her heart went pitter-pat so loudly she thought it would burst, but it was only a blackbird in the beech leaves.

When she was through the wood she stopped a few minutes to rest and nibble some sweet, short grass. She found the teasel bushes growing in the hedge, among some nettles, and she bit off three prickly heads and put them in her basket.

Then, with a laugh of delight, she ran on till she

got to the Farmer's garden. She passed the hole in the wall, for the gate was open, so in she tripped, over the lettuce and under the rhubarb to the carrot bed.

'I wish we could grow carrots at home,' she said, as she pulled them up one by one and placed them carefully in her basket. 'I don't like to come here, I am so afraid of the netting. If only Hare would eat lettuce, it would be so much easier,' and she gave a little sigh.

Swish! Swish! A sack was thrown over her and someone hit wildly at her with a rake.

Little Grey Rabbit ran this way and that, in the dark, making no noise, holding her breath, her eyes starting with fear, as she tried to dodge the blows. One hit the basket and nearly broke it, and hurt her paw, but still she ran. Then she found a gap, and out she darted, dodging in and out of the cabbage leaves, with the Farmer running after, close to her heels.

'You little rascal,' he called, 'you've been after my carrots. Just wait till I catch you.'

But little Grey Rabbit did not wait. She could not stop to explain that she thought they were everybody's carrots, and that she wanted them for Hare. No, she ran for her life, through the gate, across the field, down the lane, and across another field to the wood.

At the edge of the wood she sat down, out of breath, and rested.

'I don't think I shall go there again,' she said, as she licked her hurt paw, and put a dock-leaf bandage over it. 'We must grow our own carrots. I will ask Wise Owl how to do it.'

But Wise Owl lived in the wood, and he was only to be seen at night. Dare she venture with that cruel Weasel waiting to catch anyone out late?

She hurried through the wood as softly as she had come, and reached home safely.

'What a long time you have been,' grumbled the Hare. 'Did you get my carrots?'

'Yes, here they are,' answered little Grey Rabbit, opening her basket and showing the young, juicy, red carrots.

'Did you get my teasel brush?' asked the Squirrel.

'I got three,' said Grey Rabbit, 'one for you and two for the store cupboard.'

She cooked the dinner, gathered the firewood, and then sat down to dry some herbs and prepare for the next day. One little pot she filled with dried daisies for tea, another with dried dandelion for puddings, another with dried wild sage for coffee, and a big pot with crab-apples for jam. She was such a busy little Rabbit she was never still a moment, but the Hare and the Squirrel sat one on each side of the fire and never moved except to put fresh wood on the blaze.

Night fell and they all went to bed, after locking and bolting the door and fastening the shutters. But when the moon shone in and the stars were twinkling, the little Grey Rabbit crept downstairs and opened the door. The moon was big in the sky and the stars winked and smiled.

She stepped out on to the dewy grass, and closed the door softly.

Everywhere was silver white. Leaves and grass sparkled and a thousand sweet scents rose to her little twitching nostrils. How delicious it was! Although she felt afraid of the Weasel, lurking like a wolf in the wood, she could not help turning head over heels and standing on her head for joy. She felt so young and free!

She jumped the brook three times in her excitement, and then trotted off to the wood. Her feet left a trail of footprints in the grass, so she turned round and walked backwards. Hopping and skipping and turning her head, twisting and twining in and out of the trees, laughing to herself she went, with no adventure except a collision with a Pheasant, who rose screaming with fright.

At last she reached the Wise Owl's house, a hollow oak tree. He sat on a bough with shining eyes searching the wood, waiting to start out on his hunt for food.

Little Grey Rabbit quickly waved a white handkerchief for a truce, and he nodded down at her.

'Wise Owl,' she began, 'will you tell me how to grow carrots like those in the farmer's garden?'

'What will you give me?' asked the Wise Owl, in a high, crying voice.

'Oh, dear, I haven't anything,' she faltered, looking very sad.

'Yes you have,' cried the Owl. 'You can give me your tail.'

'My tail, my little tail, my white tail that I've had ever since I was born?' she exclaimed in horror.

'Yes, your tail, or I shall not help you.'

Little Grey Rabbit twisted round and looked at her tail. How pretty it was, so soft and fluffy and white! How lonely she would be without it! But if she went again to the Farmer's garden she might lose her life. Better to lose her tail.

'You can have it,' she cried bravely, 'but be quick.'

The Wise Owl hopped down and with one bite of his strong beak he cut if off. Then he fastened it on his front door as a door-knocker.

The Grey Rabbit put her teeth together and did not cry, but it hurt her very much. Wise Owl was not so bad after all, for he wrapped a cobweb round the stump, and it soon healed.

'You can grow carrots,' said he solemnly, as he returned to the bough, 'with seed. It isn't grass seed, nor daisy seed, nor dandelion seed, it is carrot seed.'

'Where can I get it?' asked the Grey Rabbit.

'From the shop at the edge of the village, where the Old Woman who is cross-eyed lives.'

'And when shall I get it?' said she faintly.

'Every afternoon after dinner the Old Dame falls asleep and you must get into the shop then.'

'But how shall I know it from dandelion seed, and daisy seed, and—?'

But Wise Owl had flapped his wings and flown away.

The little Grey Rabbit started home again, walking quietly now in the bright moonlight, for she missed her tail. She stepped into her own footprints which she could easily trace, but now and then a shiny round tear fell on the grass, and she gave a sigh.

Everything was quiet, for Wise Owl was flying

over the wood; she could see his shadow as he sailed silently over the tree-tops, hunting. She knew he would not touch her.

Suddenly, as she turned a corner, she saw the Weasel standing in her path. His back was turned, he was examining the footprints.

'Ah!' cried he, 'a Rabbit has gone this way,' and he ran along in front of her. Little Grey Rabbit's heart banged and thumped as she followed a long way behind, yet keeping him in sight.

When he came to the brook he was puzzled, and Grey Rabbit watched. At this side of the water the footprints went to the water's edge, but at the other side, too, they went towards the edge. He scratched his whiskers.

'She must have tumbled in and been drowned,'

said he, and he went off down the stream, hunting and sniffing.

Grey Rabbit leapt over, ran to the house, upstairs and into bed, where she slept and slept till the birds began to sing.

'That Weasel has been round the house in the night,' said the Hedgehog as he delivered the milk the next morning. 'I saw his footprints this morning, by your door.'

'Whatever have you done with your tail?' said the Hare, staring at her as she bustled about getting breakfast.

'Grey Rabbit, where *is* your tail?' echoed the Squirrel, frowning at her.

'I gave it to Wise Owl,' said Grey Rabbit, blushing and hanging her head.

'Disgraceful,' said the Hare.

'Disgracefuller,' said the Squirrel, not to be outdone.

A big tear ran down into her tea, and splashed her cuffs. She felt very unhappy, and wished Wise Owl would give her back her tail.

After dinner that day she took her basket and started off on her journey, leaving the two sitting dozing one on each side of the fire. They did not see her go, neither did they see the window open stealthily, and a black nose appear.

Little Grey Rabbit turned in another direction, and did not cross the brook. She went down the lane, overhung with honeysuckle and blackberry

bushes, and as she walked along she cheered up to see the birds fluttering about their nests.

A horse and cart went by, and a mare cantered down the lane, but she stepped aside and stood by the hedge, and no one saw her.

When she came to the village it was very quiet, for the children were in school and the labourers had gone back to work in the fields. Dogs lay asleep on doorsteps, and cats basked in the sun.

No one saw a little Grey Rabbit with a little grey shadow slip down the road, hesitate a moment outside the village shop, and then run through the open door.

'What a good thing the door was open,' she thought. 'Whatever should I have done?'

She gazed about her with wide-open eyes. Wonderful things lay all about. Buckets and frying-pans, pots and cheeses, mouse-traps and cherry brandy. She was bewildered as she looked for the seeds.

The Old Lady sat behind the counter, with her head on one side and her spectacles dropping off.

Her regular snores at first startled the Grey Rabbit, who nearly ran away, thinking it was some fierce animal, but as the Old Lady never moved she plucked up her courage and went on with the hunt.

Would she ever find it? Tins of tongue, bacon, mending wool, lollipops. Then she saw the picture of a carrot on a little packet, lying among other packets in a basket near her feet. She picked it up, smelled it, shook it, and put it in her basket.

Success at last! Grey Rabbit picked up some more packets, and looked at the bright pictures. What a treasure! Here were lettuces and radishes, parsley, cabbages, poppies and mignonette.

Quickly she seized one of each kind. Then she saw a bag with a yellow bird on it, labelled 'Canary Seed', so she took that too.

'I will plant that seed and have some little yellow birds as well as carrots in the garden,' she thought.

The bag was heavy, and as she dragged it into

the basket she made a noise which awoke the Old Lady.

'Thieves! Thieves! Maria, Sally, come quickly. Help!!'

Grey Rabbit picked up the basket and fled for the door, but not before the Old Lady had seen her.

'What is the matter, mother?' asked her daughters, hurrying in from their washing-up in the kitchen.

'A rabbit! A rabbit's gone off with something,' she gasped.

How they laughed at her and teased her! They said she had been dreaming. 'Mother's Rabbit,' they said ever after, when she made a mistake.

The little Grey Rabbit ran down the street as if an army were after her, but all was still, and, except for five ducks which waddled across the road, and rudely called after her, 'Go it, little 'un,' she saw no one.

The journey home was pleasant, and she made plans as she tripped along in and out of the shadows.

'I shall dig up that bit of grass under the hedge and pick out the stones. Then I shall sow three rows of carrot seeds. I shall sow radishes next to them, and parsley next. I will dig that good piece in the middle for the bird seed, and when the young yellows come out they will make nests in the hedge and live with the robins.'

'Ah,' she went on, getting more and more delighted with her plans, 'I may get hundreds and hundreds of little birds from this bag of seed, and hundrĕds of carrots from this packet, and hundreds of radishes from this, and hundreds — Goodness me, whatever is this?'

For she had reached home and the door stood wide open. No one was within. Upstairs she ran, in the bedrooms, in the attic and the box-room. No one was there. In the kitchen the chairs were upset and the table pushed on one side. Bits of red hair from Squirrel's tail lay on the floor, and the sleeve of Hare's coat lay dirty in a corner.

'Oh, my dear Squirrel, my darling Hare,' she

cried, with tears running down her cheeks. 'Has that bad Weasel got you?'

She took a pair of scissors, a rope, and a stick, and stared out to look for her companions.

Over the brook she found the trace of the Weasel, and at one side the grass was flattened and flowers were broken as if a heavy object had been dragged along.

'He has put them in a bag and dragged them home,' she murmured, as she examined the track. 'Poor, poor things! I do hope they are alive. If only I hadn't stopped so long choosing bird seed.'

She hurried along the path, which took her through dark and gloomy glades, and brought her to an ugly black house, with the shutters up and nettles and weeds growing in the garden. She walked round it, glancing to right and left, but heard nothing.

Then she lay down under a bush and waited. A thick black smoke came out of the chimney, and she could hear the crackle of sticks. The door opened and a great savage Weasel stood on the doorstep.

'I shall need some more sticks after all,' he said aloud. 'They will be safe in there.'

He shut the door and turned the key in the lock. Then he ran about among the bushes picking up sticks.

Grey Rabbit was very much frightened. If she stayed where she was she might be seen, if she

went out she might be caught.

'Too-whit, Too-whoo,' called an Owl over-head, and the Weasel looked up. He stood gazing up into the trees, for he was afraid of Wise Owl, and he dared not move. The Owl saw Grey Rabbit, and knew her as the owner of his door-knocker.

But Grey Rabbit made a dash, seized the key, and was in the house whilst the Weasel still gazed up at the foe overhead. Then the Owl flew away, and he wiped his brow.

'That was a near thing,' said he. 'I might have been someone else's dinner, instead of going to my own excellent roast. Now what about some acorn sauce?' And he stopped to pick up a few acorns and carried them in with his wood.

Little Grey Rabbit called, 'Hare, Squirrel, where are you? It's me, it's Rabbit.'

'Here, here; O, save us, dear Grey Rabbit,' cried two piteous voices from a bag under the sofa.

Quickly Rabbit cut it open and let the two unhappy ones out, but they were so bruised and weak they could hardly walk.

'Hare for lunch, and Squirrel for tea,
With acorn sauce is a feast for me,'

sang a rough voice, as the Weasel came home.

'Upstairs with you,' cried Grey Rabbit, 'and take this rope. Let yourselves out by the window and get home. I will follow. Quick,' and she bundled them upstairs.

Then she seized a three-legged stool which stood on the hearth, and crept into the bag with it.

'Squirrel for lunch and Hare for tea,
And bones for supper is good for me,'

shouted the Weasel as he threw down the wood, and kicked the bag in passing.

Grey Rabbit squeaked and moaned, and the Weasel chuckled. He piled the wood on the fire until the flames licked up the chimney, and the room was full of dancing shadows and smoke. Grey Rabbit lay watching him through the hole and waiting for a chance. Upstairs Squirrel and

Hare were very busy. They fastened the rope to a bed-post and then slid down into the nettles. It was easy for Squirrel, but Hare was fat, and he bumped and bruised himself still more as he swung against the house.

Away they limped, struggling through the bushes, over brambles and across ditches, for the Weasel's house was in the midst of the wildest, thickest wood.

Weasel opened the oven door and took down a large tin.

'I'll roast them both together,' he muttered, for like many lonely people he had a habit of talking aloud.

He put some dripping in the tin to get hot. Then he took a stick and came to the bag. He dragged it out, and pinched Grey Rabbit as he did so. He raised the stick, and, Bang! down it came. Grey Rabbit crept inside the stool and lay protected by its legs.

'Oh! Oh!' she cried, once like Hare, and once like Squirrel.

Bang! he went again.

'Oh! Oh!' she cried more feebly.

Bang! he went once more.

'Oh! Oh!' she cried very weakly.

Bang! Bang! he went on the stool legs, but there was never a sound.

'Dead, both dead,' said the Weasel. 'Now is the oven ready?'

He opened the oven door and took hold of the hot tin. It was heavy, and he took both paws to lift it. Like a flash, Grey Rabbit slipped out of the bag, picked up the stool, and gave him a great push into the tin. Then she shut the oven door.

Off she ran, not stopping to hear his cries, but running as if he were after her. She never stopped till she got home, and as she sat panting in an armchair, the other two limped in.

'Oh, Grey Rabbit,' they both said, 'we want to tell you we are very sorry for our behaviour. We shall never be proud and rude again. We have had our lesson. You saved us from the Weasel, and if ever he comes here again—'

'He won't, he is roasted by now.' she interrupted. Then she told all her adventures.

'Grey Rabbit,' said Squirrel solemnly, shaking her paw for emphasis, 'you shall always have the rocking-chair, and sit by the fire. You shall have your breakfast in bed, you shall have toast and coffee.'

'Grey Rabbit,' said Hare, twitching his big ears, and staring at her with his big eyes, 'you shall have a party, by moonlight, and we will ask all the rabbits from the common to feast and dance in the garden.'

But Grey Rabbit laughed. 'I don't want to lie in bed, I like to work, and I don't want toast and coffee, but I should like to sit in the rocking-chair sometimes, and I should like a party.'

So they all lived happily together, and had a fine crop of radishes and carrots, and onions and mignonette, but no little yellow birds came up.

Sometime I will tell you how Grey Rabbit got her tail back again.

How Little
Grey Rabbit Got
Back Her Tail

One cold March morning little Grey Rabbit awoke at dawn and lay for a moment looking round her dim white-washed attic. Then she jumped out of bed, washed her face and paws, and slipped on her grey dress with its white collar and cuffs. Round her waist she tied a blue apron, for this was to be a busy day.

Softly she opened her door and listened. Snores could be heard coming from Hare's room, and squeaky little grunts from Squirrel's. They were both fast asleep!

She crept downstairs like a shadow, and went into the kitchen. From a hook she took down a round wicker basket and then she went out into the raw air.

The sun had not risen, and a star was still in the sky, 'like a candle for a little rabbit', she thought.

As she walked down the garden path she looked back at the shut windows, and waved a paw to her sleeping friends in the little house. She turned down the lane and scampered over the stones, leaping over thorny briars, and swinging her basket round and round over her head.

A startled mouse scuttled into the hedge and gazed after her with astonished eyes. 'Grey Rabbit is off early this morning,' he told his wife. 'I wonder where she is going? It's a pity she's lost her tail, she must feel cold. They say it is fastened up on Wise Owl's door, but may I never see it!' He curled his own tail round and settled down to sleep again.

The Rabbit came to an opening in a hedge, by a wildrose bush, now bare and spiny, and she climbed through, tearing her apron on a curved thorn. She stopped to pin it with a straight pin from a hawthorn bush, and to sip the water from a gurgling spring, like a small fountain in the grass.

Then she ran across the wet meadow to a bank where the first primroses were growing, with petals closed, asleep on their green leaves in the early light. She put down her basket and began to pick them, biting off their pink stalks, and putting the yellow blossoms in the basket.

Her little nose twitched with pleasure as she worked among the sweet smells, and she rubbed herself on the leaves to get the scent in her hair. When she finished there, she ran to another field, and another, and another, with a basket now heaped with petals. Behind her she left a trail of small footprints which scarcely pressed down the grey-green grass.

Suddenly a black nose and two pink hands with funny little human fingers stuck out of the earth in front of her. She started back.

'Oh! Oh! Moldy Warp, how you frightened me!' she exclaimed, with her paw on her fluttering heart. 'Wherever have you come from?'

'I was asleep, Grey Rabbit, but you woke me, pit-pattering just over my pillow, so I came out to see who it was,' and the Mole shook off the red soil clinging to his bare feet and wiped his hands on the grass.

'How are the Hare and Squirrel?' he asked politely, picking up the primroses Grey Rabbit had dropped in her fright.

'Squirrel is very well, but Hare has a bad cold. He sat in a draught last week, watching March come in like a Lion, and he has sneezed ever since.'

'What are you doing out here so early, Grey Rabbit?'

'I am picking primroses for Primrose Wine,' answered the Rabbit. 'It's a certain cure for a cold. My mother used to make it. These are the first primroses so they are the sweetest, and they will make the best wine. besides, I've picked them with the dew on them.'

'What a clever Rabbit you are!' said the Mole admiringly. 'But where is your tail?' he added, blinking his small eyes.

Grey Rabbit told how she gave her tail to Wise Owl in return for his advice on gardening.

'I didn't know Owl was a gardener,' said Moldy Warp shortly. 'I thought I was the best digger hereabouts,' and he proudly held up his hands and spread out his fingers.

'Of course you are, Moldy; there is no one like you except Badger. Owl advised me about seeds, carrot seed, lettuce seed, so that we could grow food ourselves.'

'Oh! He did, did he?' muttered the Mole, 'and he took your tail, did he?'

'No, I gave it to him,' returned Grey Rabbit sadly.

Mole and the Rabbit sat on the bank among the primrose leaves and watched the green sky with its baby pink cloudlets change as the great red sun lifted itself out of a bath of mist.

'Grey Rabbit,' said the Mole solemnly, 'would you like your tail back, very very much?'

'Very very much,' answered Grey Rabbit mournfully, 'but Owl is a kind of friend, and he must not be made my enemy.'

'I'll help you, Grey Rabbit,' said the Mole, striking his breast with his hand, just as a long level sunray shone across the field and turned his velvet waistcoat red. 'I will think out a plan and we will get it back.'

'Goodbye, and thank you, Moldy Warp,' said the Rabbit. 'I must run now, or I shall be late for breakfast,' and off she ran with her flowers bobbing up and down in the basket.

At the little house by the Wood, there was dismay when Grey Rabbit was missed. Hare ran up and downstairs with his head in a red cotton handkerchief, calling, 'Where are you, Grey Rabbit? A-tishoo! Are you hiding, Grey Rabbit? A-tishoo!'

But Squirrel saw the basket was gone, and guessed that Rabbit was busy somewhere.

'Help me to get the breakfast, Hare, instead of calling like that,' she scolded.

Hare wiped his eyes with a corner of the handkerchief, sneezed violently, and blew a bunch of camomile off the shelf. 'A-tishoo! A-tishoo!' went he, and the little brown tea-pot rocked on the table.

'Oh, do be careful!' exclaimed Squirrel. 'What will Grey Rabbit say if she finds the teapot on the floor?'

'Grey Rabbit thinks more of my cold than of the old teapot,' said Hare, as he swept the tablecloth off the table and wrapped it round his shoulders. 'She is sympa-what-do-you-call-it, and you are not.'

'No, I am not sympa-what-do-you-call-it,' said Squirrel, indignantly seizing the cloth and shaking it. She reset the table, and made a dish of

scrambled ants' eggs. She minced a bunch of grass and flavoured it with carrot and turnip from the store-house. She filled the three plates, put them on the table, and drew up the chairs.

'Rat-a-tat-tat' came Hedgehog with the milk.

'Late again! Have you seen Grey Rabbit?' asked Squirrel.

Hedgehog shook his old head. 'No,' said he, 'I've been too busy a-milking my cow. She wouldn't lie still this morning, and I had to chase her all over the field. At my time of life, too. Is little Grey Rabbit missing?'

'Of course she is or I should not ask you,' snapped the Squirrel, who began to feel anxious.

'Sorry, no offence,' said the Hedgehog, picking up his milkcan and shuffling down the path.

'I can't abide that pair,' he muttered, 'though Robin says they are a deal better since Grey Rabbit rescued them from the Weasel. Now little Grey Rabbit is a nice little thing.'

A light footstep came up the lane and a voice was heard singing:

'Primroses, primroses,
Primroses fine,
Pick them and press them,
And make yellow wine.'

The Grey Rabbit tripped up to him. 'Good morning, Hedgehog. Have you brought the milk?'

'Yes, and had my head snapped off by those two. They think another Weasel has you,' and he laughed grimly.

She opened the gate and ran to the house.

'Hare! Squirrel! Look at my primroses, a basketful, picked with the dew on them, to make Primrose Wine and cure your cold, Hare!'

'I knew she was sympa-what-do-you-call-it,' cried Hare delightedly.

All day they made the wine. Grey Rabbit packed the heads in layers in a wooden cask, tightly, and between each layer she put an acorn-cup of honey and a squeeze of wood-sorrel juice. Squirrel picked the wood-sorrel and Hare pounded it with a stone. Squirrel filled the kettle

many times from the brook, and put it on the fire. Grey Rabbit poured the boiling water over the flowers until the cask was full. Then she sealed it with melted beeswax and buried it in the garden.

'How tired I am, pounding all those leaves,' said Hare, as they sat down to tea.

'How tired I am, filling all those kettles, said Squirrel.

'How glad I am the wine is made,' said Grey Rabbit, as she poured out the tea and cut the bread and carrot.

'When can we have some?' asked Hare.

'In twenty-four hours,' said the Rabbit, and Hare began to count the minutes, and to sneeze very loudly.

That night Wise Owl flew over the house. 'Too-whit, atishoo! Too-whoo, a-tishoo!' he cried. 'Too-wishoo-oo-oo! Too-whoosh-oo-oo!'

As he flew over fields and woods there came a faint 'Tishoo-oo-oo' floating in the wind.

'Poor Wise Owl,' murmured Grey Rabbit to her blanket, 'I must take him a bottle of Primrose Wine, too.'

The next day Squirrel, dressed in a brown overall, worked in the garden, digging the soil, raking the rough little knobs with her scarlet-handled rake, and sowing fresh dandelion and lettuce seed.

Hare sat sneezing by the fire, playing noughts and crosses against himself. He always won, so he was happy. Beside, he kept thinking of the wine, and counting the minutes.

Grey Rabbit had some sewing to do. She sat in the rocking-chair making new white collars and cuffs for herself, and mending her torn apron. Then she made a red Sunday coat for Hare, and a yellow dress for Squirrel. Her needle ran in and out, and the tiny bobbins of cotton emptied themselves as she sewed, until two white, three red, and three yellow ones rolled on the brick floor.

At last she finished and put away her work. Squirrel came in, stamping her feet and crying out against the cold.

'It's bitter today, Grey Rabbit. Where's my teasel brush? It's time you got me another.'

Grey Rabbit found the brush in the wood-

scuttle, where Squirrel had thrown it.

She brushed and combed the Squirrel's tail until it was glossy and bright again. Then she picked up the bobbins, and strung them on a horse-hair ready to give to Hedgehog when he called with the milk.

After dinner she left Hare explaining how to win at noughts and crosses to Squirrel, who could never understand, and away she went over the brook and through the Wood with her basket.

The trees were bare, but here and there a honeysuckle waved tender green leaves as it climbed up a nut tree. The Rabbit stopped to taste these, and put a few in her basket to mix with the salad for supper. Next she picked some stiff little purple buds from a low-hanging elm. She looked longingly at a horse-chestnut whose sticky buds were beyond her reach.

'If only Squirrel would come into the Wood again,' said she, 'we could have such delicious meals!'

It was very quiet here; no rabbits ran among the undergrowth, no birds sang in the tree-tops, only now and then a rook flew overhead with a rough 'Caw, Caw', or a pheasant scattered the beech leaves which covered the ground. The Rabbit's heart thumped, she was always nervous in this Wood. Her ears were pressed back and her eyes looked all ways at once, but nothing came to alarm her. At last she ran through the gate and entered the teasel field. She bit off a few heads, all dry and prickly, and then she filled her basket with curling shoots of young green bracken, which she found hidden under the dead-gold fronds, and knobby fern-buds from under a wall.

Home she ran, softly through the Wood, stepping on the soft moss and mould, and avoiding the rustling leaves.

'Robin Redbreast has been with a letter for you,' said Squirrel, emptying the basket in the larder and putting the brushes in a cupboard.

Grey Rabbit took the tightly-sealed leaf-envelope, and broke open the brown flap.

'Who is it from?' asked the curious Hare.

'It's Moldy Warp's writing,' answered Rabbit, as she turned the letter up and down, inside and out.

'What does it say?' asked Squirrel.

'It says "Found Knock Mole",' said Rabbit.

'Whatever can it mean?' they all asked.

Hare said, 'Moldy Warp has been found knocked over.'

Squirrel said, 'Mr Knock has found Mole.'

Grey Rabbit said, 'Mole has found a Knock, but who has lost one?'

As the evening wore on Hare got more and more excited, until he could hardly bear to wait for Rabbit to dig up the cask.

The seals were broken and such a delicious smell came into the room, like pine forests, and honeysuckle, and lime trees in flower. Hare and Squirrel ran for their blue-rimmed mugs and dipped them in the cask. They came out filled to the brim with a golden thick syrup.

'Good! good!' said Hare, smacking his lips, 'I feel better already.'

'Beautiful!' sighed Squirrel in a rapture.

Grey Rabbit filled a bottle and tucked it under her arm. 'I'm going off at once with this bottle to Wise Owl,' said she. 'He sneezed all over the sky last night,' and before they could protest she had gone.

It was a dark night, the moon had not risen, but the stars in Orion's belt shone down and lighted her path in the black Wood, as she hurried along to the tree where Wise Owl lived. She would have to be quick to catch him before he went out hunting. The Wood was full of little sounds, rustles

45

and murmurs. What were they? Grey Rabbit did not know; she only felt very frightened, for they were not comfortable homely sounds. She looked up at the blinking stars, and the way seemed clearer.

'A-tishoo! A-tishoo! Tishoo!' came echoing through the trees, and she caught sight of Owl's shining eyes, and her own little white tail hanging on the door of the big oak tree.

'Is it lonely too?' she wondered.

She waved her handkerchief as a truce, and Wise Owl nodded to her. 'A-tishoo! A-tishoo!' said he.

'Wise Owl, I've brought you some Primrose Wine for your sneeze,' said she.

He hopped down and took the bottle from her trembling paw.

'Thank you, Grey Rabbit, thank you kindly,' and, opening wide his beak, he drank all the wine and then swallowed the bottle.

'That's good! Even old Owl could not make

Primrose Wine. What would you like, Grey Rabbit?'

She hesitated and looked at her forlorn tail.

'No, Grey Rabbit, I could not part with that, unless you bring me a bell to go ting-a-ling-a-ling when visitors call. Then you shall have it. But here is a book of riddles.'

He gave her a little green book of Owlish jokes.

'But, Wise Owl, where shall I find a bell?' said poor Grey Rabbit, who sadly wanted her tail.

'In the a-tishoo! The world is full of bells and a-tishoos,' sneezed Wise Owl, and he raised his great wings, and flew over the Wood.

Grey Rabbit ran home again with the book in her paw, but her thoughts full of the bell. The murmurs in the Wood became fainter as Owl flew over, and now the white moon, beloved of all rabbits, was slowly rising over the hill.

Squirrel and Hare were sitting up for her, with a mug of mulled wine on the hob, and between them, sipping from a tea-cup, sat the Mole.

'Here she comes! here she comes!' they cried, as the latch rattled and she flung open the door.

'Mole has something for you,' said Hare excitedly.

Mole brought out a large silver penny, with an eagle on one side and an emperor on the other.

'It's Roman,' he said. 'I found it deep down in the earth, and I thought it would do for Wise Owl's door-knocker.'

'Oh, you kind Moldy Warp! Do you mean instead of my tail? Alas! Wise Owl wants a bell; he will give it to me for a bell.'

'A bell? A bell? Where can we get a bell?'

'A bell rings people to church,' said Hare.

'There is a bell in the village shop,' said Grey Rabbit.

'A bell calls the children to school,' said Squirrel.

'There are Hare-bells, Blue-bells and Canterbury-bells,' said Hare.

'I might make a bell,' said the Mole, holding the penny in his strong hands. 'I will bend it and bend it and twist it with my fingers till—' and he walked musingly out of the house.

'Good night, good night,' everyone called after him, but he only said, 'And bend it and twist it and bend it,' as he went slowly down the garden path with the moonlight on his silver penny.

Hare took the book of riddles to bed with him, and prepared to astonish Squirrel with a joke. But when he awoke without his a-tishoo, he felt so grateful to Grey Rabbit that he got up early, and went out into the fields to look for bells.

When Grey Rabbit had filled the little blue-rimmed mugs with milk, and put the dandelion leaves on a dish, the nuts on a plate, and the salad of buds in a bowl, she called Hare.

'Hare, Hare, come to breakfast.'

Hare came scampering in. 'I've been looking

for Hare-bells,' said he, 'but the Spinks say there are no Hare-bells in March, and they called me a March Hare for looking for them.'

'I'm going to the village shop to get that bell,' announced Squirrel.

'Oh, Squirrel!' exclaimed Grey Rabbit, 'please don't. The old woman might catch you.'

'That she never will,' laughed Squirrel, but secretly she was frightened at her own daring.

After dinner, when the old woman had her nap, Squirrel started off. She put on her best yellow dress, and her little blue shoes, and she tried her tail with a bow of blue ribbon.

'You never know who will see me,' she said, as she admired herself in the glass.

'Run for your life if anyone does see you,' said Hare warningly.

She ran with a hop and a skip down the lane, leaping over budding brambles, stopping now and then to eat a green sycamore bud. Under the brambles white violets were hiding in their bunches of leaves, and she picked a small bunch.

She entered the village, and found all quiet, except for an old Farmer, jogging home behind his brown mare.

She ran swiftly across the empty market-place to the shop, but the door was shut, so she hid in a garden near.

Presently a woman came out of the cottage and pushed open the shop door. Tinkle, tinkle, went the bell.

'It's still there,' said Squirrel, running in after her.

'A pound of candles, please, Mrs Bunting,' said the woman. 'And how's your cough?'

'It might be better, Mrs Snowball, and it might be worse,' said Mrs Bunting, reaching for the candles.

'Well,' said Mrs Snowball, 'you should get an onion, and boil it, and then bake it, and then mix it with—' But her sentence was never finished, for the Squirrel, crying, 'Death or Glory', leapt at the bell, and tugged and bit and pushed.

The two women shrieked as the jangling bell banged violently backwards and forwards with a yellow animal swinging on it.

50

'It's a monkey, a great yellow monkey,' cried one.

'No, it's a wild cat, a great yellow wild cat, with a blue ribbon,' shouted the other, and they both ran screaming to the Blacksmith next door.

Squirrel kicked her shoes off and lost her blue bow, but she forced the bell, and fell with it to the floor, knocking over three buckets, a milkcan, a mouse-trap, and a basket of eggs. Such a din and clatter came from the shop! Squirrel picked up the bell and ran out of the door, jingling-jangling through the market-place.

'There it is, there it is, Mr Blacksmith. That's the creature and it's got my bell,' cried Mrs Bunting.

The Blacksmith threw a hammer after Squirrel, which hit the bell, making it ring even more.

'My daughters will say it was another rabbit, when they come home,' said Mrs Bunting angrily.

'It's my opinion it was a squirrel, ma'am,' said the Blacksmith mildly, but when Mrs Bunting found a bunch of violets and a pair of tiny blue shoes, he scratched his head and said, 'It's mighty queer!'

Away went Squirrel, dragging the noisy bell with its coil of thick springs twisting round her tail. Such a rattle was never heard, and the dogs and the cats awoke, barking and howling. She passed the old brown mare, who shied in a fright and nearly upset the farmer out of the cart. She banged and bumped along the road, up the lane, through the garden, and into the house.

Squirrel was a heroine that day.

But when Hare and Grey Rabbit dragged the bell across the Wood to Wise Owl's door, he put out his head with half-shut eyes and hooted.

'Who's waking up all the Wood? How can I catch any dinner with that hullabaloo? How can I sleep with that jingle-jangle? Take it away!' And he banged his door, so that the little white tail shook.

They left the bell to rust in the Wood, and ages afterwards it was found by a gamekeeper, who returned it to Mrs Bunting.

When the dejected Hare and Grey Rabbit got home they found Mole talking to Squirrel. He had brought a silver bell, a little bigger than a Hare-bell, a little less than a Foxglove-bell, with a tiny clapper of a hawthorn stone, hung on a hair from a white mare's tail.

When he shook it a sweet silvery tinkle came from it, so delicate so thin, so musical, that Squirrel and Hare looked round to see if a Jenny Wren was in the room, and Grey Rabbit looked out to see if the stars were singing.

All round the bell Moldy Warp had made a pattern of lines like a shell, and in the middle the eagle spread his wings. They hung up the bell by its twist of sheep's wool, and listened to the song of bees and flowers and rippling sunny leaves, and deep moss which it sang to them.

Grey Rabbit started off with it as soon as it was dusk. She felt no fear as she carried it tinkling through the thick Wood, for the Wood held its breath to listen.

'What is that?' asked Wise Owl, as he peered down from his branch, and moved his small ears.

'A bell for my tail,' said Grey Rabbit boldly, and she tinkled the little silver bell.

Owl climbed down.

'You shall have your tail, Grey Rabbit. Give me the bell. It is soft,' he went on, 'no one can hear it but our own people. It is beautiful, for it is like a flower. It is wise, for it lived in the beginning of the world.'

So he hung up the bell on his front door, and there it sang with every breeze. And he gave Grey Rabbit her soft white tail in exchange. He fastened it on with threads of Stitch-wort, and anointed it with the Herb of St John, so that by the time Grey Rabbit reached home again her tail was as good as ever.

But Moldy Warp took with him to his house under the green fields a bottle of Primrose Wine and the thanks of the little company.

The Great Adventure of Hare

It was a lovely midsummer morning, and Hare looked out of his bedroom window on to the fields where cloud shadows were running races. Gentle blue butterflies and fierce little wasps flew among the flowers in the garden below. Hare stroked his whiskers and said, 'Just the day for my adventure.'

'Grey Rabbit, Grey Rabbit, come here,' he called over the banisters, 'and bring my walking-stick, will you?'

A scamper of little feet echoed on the brick floor in the kitchen, and Grey Rabbit ran upstairs with a cherrywood stick and a teasel-brush. Hare took down his new blue coat from the hook behind the bedroom door. He put it on, with Grey Rabbit's help, twisting his head to get a good view of the two brass buttons at the back. Grey Rabbit brushed off some tiny specks of white-wash with her teasel. She had to stand on tiptoes to reach his shoulders, she was so small.

'Are my buttons all right?' asked Hare.

'Yes, like two looking-glasses,' replied Grey

Rabbit, as she gave each one a rub with a duster, and then peeped at her face in the dazzling buttons.

'Don't forget your watch,' she added, as the Hare started downstairs.

'Oh dear, how careless you are, Grey Rabbit,' said the Hare, taking a large flat silver watch from the chest of drawers, and putting it in his waistcoat pocket. 'I nearly went without it.'

'It's late,' he continued, 'half-past twelve.'

'Half-past seven by the sun,' said Grey Rabbit, quietly.

'The sun's five hours slow,' returned Hare, as he walked downstairs, and Grey Rabbit stopped behind to hang up his old blue coat, which lay crumpled on the floor.

'Goodbye, Squirrel,' called Hare, as Squirrel looked up from the mittens she was knitting. 'Goodbye, I'm off on my great journey. Goodbye, Grey Rabbit, I shall be back for supper, and mind there is something nice.'

He stepped out of the little door into the sunshine.

'Take care of yourself,' cried Grey Rabbit, running after him and waving her paw. 'Mind the traffic, and give Toad our present.'

'Don't forget to bring a present back,' called Squirrel.

'I will bring presents for all three of us,' replied Hare, importantly, as he marched down the garden path, with his head in the air, and his buttons flashing.

He was going to visit the famous Toad who lived in the Ash Wood, at the other side of the wide valley. Squirrel had laughed when he said he was going, and said, 'You never dare.'

'Daresen't I?' he replied. 'You'll see!'

Grey Rabbit had looked a little anxious, but she was pleased that the timid Hare was so bold.

She decided to give the house a summer-cleaning whilst he was away. So Squirrel took her knitting up an apple tree to be out of the way, and Little Grey Rabbit, with scrubbing brush and pail, prepared to clean the rooms.

Hare shut the garden gate with a bang, and flicked his handkerchief at three flies who seemed determined to travel with him. He picked a sprig of sweet marjoram from the bush outside the gate, put it in his buttonhole, and prepared to leap over the brook.

But he changed his mind, and sat down by the water, turning this way and that to see his buttons. As he twisted and craned his neck, a mocking voice cried, 'Haven't you gone yet? You'll never get to Ash Wood if you don't start,' and he saw Squirrel's face peering down from the apple tree.

Hare sprang up and marched off pretending not to hear. He entered the big wood where Wise Owl lived.

All was quiet there, and the flies deserted him to find another traveller going some happier way. He held his stick firmly and whistled softly as he walked warily, fearfully, on the soft moss. His eyes looked at each side, and his ears, pricked back, kept guard behind. He was so intent on this sideways and backward glance that he did not see where he was going, and suddenly he bumped into a scared rabbit, who also was looking behind him.

With cries of alarm they both fell head over heels. The Rabbit picked himself up, muttering, 'Silly old Clumsy', and ran on. Hare brushed his coat, and picked off some old leaves which clung to it. He examined his watch, and searched for his stick which had fallen into a blackberry bush.

A sound came from behind a tree, and a Cock Pheasant walked out with proudly lifted legs.

'Good morning, Pheasant,' said the Hare. 'It's a fine day today. I've just had a tumble—some stupid rabbit, not looking where he was going.'

'Hush,' whispered the Pheasant. 'Don't talk so loudly, young fellow.'

'Why, what's the matter? Don't you live here?' asked Hare.

'No, my home is in the glade yonder,' said the Pheasant, pointing with one foot to a clearing which showed light among the dense trees, 'but I don't want these fellows to know. Too many shady people in this wood. Break open a house, rob, no respect for property. Only last week I had my water-butt emptied and my larder ransacked by a thief.'

'Who was it, do you think?' asked Hare.

'It was Jay; he left a bit of his blue scarf behind him.'

'He daren't come to our house,' said Hare.

'You never know. There are other robbers besides Jay. Don't boast till you are out of the wood,' and saying this, the Pheasant flew away with a heavy flap of his wings.

Hare ran on until he came to a great oak tree with a little door, and a silver bell hanging by a thin rope.

'Should I? Should I? Should I ring Moldy Warp's bell?' thought he. 'Suppose Owl should come. What could I say? I'll ask the way to Ash Wood.'

He pulled the string, and 'Tinkle, tinkle', sang the tiny bell. Hare got ready to run, but a sleepy voice called, 'What do you want, Hare?' and Owl looked out, blinking in the sunlight.

Hare faltered, 'Er – er – er – which way is the way to Ash Wood, please, Wise Owl?'

The Owl looked down severely, and Hare quickly got out his silk handkerchief from his coat pocket and waved it violently.

'What do you mean by waking me up for such a question? Where is your money?'

Hared started, remembering how little Grey Rabbit had lost her tail; but Owl had seen the shining buttons.

'I'll take those buttons from the back of your coat,' said he, and he clambered down, and cut them off before Hare could say 'Jigger-jagger'.

'Go through the wood, cross the teasel-field, turn to the right through the village, to the left across the railway line, up the fields, through Bilberry Wood, past Home Farm, and the Ash Wood is at the top of the hill,' said the Owl, all in one breath.

'Thank you,' muttered Hare, retreating.

'A Fox lives in Bilberry Wood,' called Wise Owl, and Hare turned pale.

'I think I shall go home,' said he.

Owl had already climbed upstairs again, and shut the door. He took some sealing wax and stuck the buttons on his night-cap, before he went to sleep.

Overhead a loud screaming laugh startled Hare, who stood undecided and alarmed. A blue Jay, who had been listening, flew by.

'Ha ha! ha ha! Frightened Hare! Timid Hare!' he mocked.

Hare grabbed his stick, straightened his shoulders, and began to whistle, 'Rule Britannia', which annoyed the Jay, and off he went.

'I expect the Fox won't notice me. I'm a pretty fast runner,' said he.

He ran through the seeding blue-bells, and purple foxgloves, flowering under the nut trees and great oaks. He ran down the stony path, where ants laboured among the patches of yellow pimpernel, under the roof of beech and elm, to the gate at the end of the wood.

In the teasel-field were red butterflies with their little baskets, gathering honey from the rag-wort, brown bumble bees, eager to talk to anyone, busy hoverflies, with no time to spare, red-caped ladybirds, and field mice in bonnets and shawls, running on errands, strolling home, gossiping by the tiny green paths, playing on swings and roundabouts, chattering and singing. It was such a busy world after the quiet wood. Hare walked across the field swinging his stick, feeling very

important in his bright coat among all these little people. He nodded to strangers, and talked to acquaintances.

What nice fellows these were! They all knew Little Grey Rabbit, for she got her teasel-brushes here, and Hare answered many kind inquiries about her.

'Where are you going, stranger?' asked a Brown Rabbit.

'To Ash Wood, to visit Toad,' answered Hare, pompously.

'My! You are a traveller!' exclaimed the Rabbit, admiringly.

'I am that,' said Hare, who seldom went beyond the garden gate.

'What other countries have you seen?' inquired the Rabbit, and three others came close to listen.

'Well – er – I've seen too many to tell you about today. I am a very famous Hare.'

They pressed closer and stared at him with wide, innocent eyes.

'I'm so famous,' continued Hare, 'that I'm called – or be be exact, I shall be called, after this journey, "Columbus Hare". That's a travelling name. Columbus was a Hare who crossed rivers, and fields, and woods, till he found another country where black rabbits lived.'

'Will you tell us about Ash Wood and Toad when you come back, Columbus Hare?'

'That I will, and I'll bring you a piece of grey ashen wood, to show I've been there, if you meet me at' – here he consulted his watch – 'at half-past twelve.'

'There's a fox in Bilberry Wood, I've been told by my wife's brother,' said a quiet little Hedgehog who had come up.

'I'm not afraid of a fox,' cried Hare, boldy, and he threw his stick up in the air and caught it.

The Rabbits gazed admiringly at him.

'Is that a magic on your chain?' asked a very small Rabbit timidly, stretching up a paw to the watch.

'Yes, it's a great magic. It's better than the Sun,' said Hare.

He sat on a stone by the clear tinkling spring which jutted out of the earth like a baby fountain, and ran down the sloping field among pink centaury and short green reeds. The Rabbits and the Hedgehog sat by him, and two Water Wagtails, chattering and merry, joined the company.

Hare picked a bunch of reeds and wove a green basket for the Wagtails. The Hedgehog dabbled in the spring with his little hands, and the Rabbits played 'Here we go round the blackberry-bush'.

Then Hare got out his sandwiches and divided them among his new friends, who were proud to sit down with such a bold adventurer.

After they had eaten even the lettuce leaves in which the food was wrapped, Hare sent them away. He curled himself up in a patch of warm long grass in the middle of the bushes, he put his two paws under his nose, and fell asleep.

He was awakened by the youngest Rabbit who

tugged at his watch. Hare sprang up in a hurry;
he had slept longer than he intended.

'Be off, you naughty child,' he scolded, and she
scuttled home to her mother.

He left the field by a gap in the hedge, crossed
the dusty lane, and ran along the narrow road
through the village.

A tortoiseshell cat arched her back and spat at
him, and a dog barked and tugged at his chain. A

baby opened his eyes very wide, and pointed at
him, and an old man fumbled in his pocket for his
spectacles to stare at him.

He leapt the limestone wall, and crossed
the field to the railway. The gleaming hot rails
burnt his toes, and the roar of a distant train
terrified him, as·he scampered across and hid in
the grass at the other side whilst the express
rushed by.

'That's a Dragon,' said he, mopping his head.

'I must be in China. I *shall* have some adventures to talk about when I get home.'

He climbed up a steep path into a rocky wood, 'on the edge of the world', thought he.

Great cool spaces were about him, and a green roof above, held up by trees like pillars. The softest moss covered the rocks lying about on the ground, and bilberry bushes, jewelled with pink flowers, grew by the path. The sun shone through the lacy boughs and dappled his fur and blue coat with yellow circles. The air was so cold and fresh, like a drink of spring water.

'Can you tell me the time?' asked a silken voice, and Hare saw a fine gentleman in a red coat sitting on a fallen tree.

'Half-past twelve,' said Hare, consulting his watch.

'Really? As early as that? Will you do me the favour of joining me in a bottle of cherry brandy?' asked the polite gentleman, and he brought out a bottle from his pocket.

'Thank you,' said Hare, regretfully, 'I am late for an appointment, but I shall be glad to join you on my way back.'

'I will wait here for you,' said the gentleman in red, smiling at Hare, 'and perhaps you would like to see my collection of birds' eggs?'

'Delighted,' said Hare, who was flattered by this notice.

'I am a bit of a collector myself. I collect

Noughts and Crosses. I won't forget,' and he trotted on, whilst the fine gentleman gazed longingly after him.

There was a curious smell which disturbed Hare. It wasn't mignonette, or lavender, or sausages, or fried eggs. 'It must be some foreign scent on his handkerchief,' thought Hare.

He picked a branch of honeysuckle and twined it round his head, and held his sprig of marjoram to his nose, but the smell remained until he left the wood and crossed the fields to the stone farm on the high ridge.

Dappled cows stood under the trees, swishing their tails as they waited to be milked. Two great mares rubbed noses as they talked about their foals, and a score of hens chattered excitedly about the Fox, who, the night before, had tried to open the hen-house door. Hare loped by without speaking, he was an outsider in this intimate company.

In front of him lay Ash Wood, with its grey trees and rustling leaves.

Apple-green moths and honey-bees came to meet him as he entered. The flowers grew in groups, a patch of red campion here, a clump of forget-me-nots there, bugle, ground-ivy, and tall bell-flowers, in their blues and purples, like mists on the ground.

'Herbs for old Toad, I suppose,' said Hare to himself, as he looked round. 'He does a lot of doctoring, they say.'

In the middle of the wood was a bog, fragrant with many coloured orchids, and there, perched on an island, was a small house with a roof thatched with rushes. Over it hung a willow, and round it, half concealing the roof, were bushes of bog-myrtle.

'Who's there?' boomed a voice, as Hare waded through the bog with his coat-tails turned up.

'It's Hare, from Grey Rabbit's house, over the valley,' said Hare.

The little door opened slowly and an immense Toad waddled out, leaning on a crutch. His eyes were bright as green lamps, and his cheeks were wrinkled with age.

He wore a green coat and yellow breeches, old and creased, but Hare felt a shabby nobody when he looked at the wise animal.

'I have brought a present,' said Hare, as the Toad gazed at him without speaking.

He searched all his pockets, dipping into one side and then the other. He hunted and hunted, and then took off his coat. He looked in his waist-coat pockets, but it wasn't there.

The toad stood, still leaning on his crutch, whilst the flustered Hare turned everything inside out.

'Here it is,' he cried at last. 'Grey Rabbit stitched it inside my coat-lining lest I should lose it on the way.' He cut the stitches and brought out an egg-beater.

'It's to beat eggs, whip them, you know, make them frothy,' explained Hare breathlessly. 'We thought it would be useful.'

Toad was entranced. For all his learning he had seen nothing like it. He held it between his knees and turned the handle so that the wheels whizzed. Then he held it in the bog so that the water frothed and foamed. He took up a handful and sipped it. 'Lemonade,' said he.

He whizzed it in a bowl of cream which stood

on the doorstep. The cream foamed in a white-ness.

'Butter,' said he.

'Come in, come in, Hare,' he cried, throwing open the little door; and, stooping very low, Hare entered the cool-flagged hall and walked through to a courtyard, where a fountain played.

Toad beat up the fountain and made rainbows of light.

Then he rang a hare-bell, and two Frogs appeared.

'Bring refreshments for this gentleman,' he commanded, 'and a bowl of wood-pigeons' eggs.'

The two Frogs returned with red wine and saffron cake which Hare ate greedily. The Toad beat up the eggs, mixed them with the wine, and made wonderful drinks which astonished Hare.

'I have no teeth,' he explained. 'It's a most useful gift, most useful. I have never been so pleased.'

He took Hare to a cupboard which was crammed with odds and ends picked up in the woods. There were skipping ropes, shuttle-cocks, rings, and pebbles, tin cans and ginger-beer bottles, kettles, mouth-organs, matches – all the things that picnickers had left behind.

'Choose a present for yourself, and one for each of your friends,' said Toad, and Hare hunted among the medley to find something suitable.

He chose a tiny pair of slippers made from the bark of the silver birch, which some rabbit had lost, for Little Grey Rabbit, and a boxwood flute, which a blackbird had dropped, for Squirrel, and a penknife with a corkscrew for himself.

Then Toad unlocked a secret drawer and took out a small green bottle labelled VENOM.

'I shall give you a bottle of my famous Venom,' said he, 'but take great care of it. You had better give it to Grey Rabbit to put in the medicine cupboard, ready for any Dangerous Visitors.'

'But Weasel is dead,' said Hare, taking it gingerly.

'You never know what may happen,' said Toad, wisely, and Hare put it in his pocket, with the slippers, flute and knife.

As Hare waded through the bog he turned round and saw the Toad busily beating the air with the egg-beater, catching the gossamer cobwebs in its wheels and twisting them into a fishnet.

'I should never have thought of that,' he said, and he stopped to pick some grey ash twigs for the Rabbits.

It was dusk when he ran across the fields to Bilberry Wood, and a little crescent moon hung in the sky. His heart was as light as his heels, and he raced along singing:

'Are you there, Mr Moon? Are you there?
Have a care, Mr Moon, here's a Hare.
Columbus, Mr Moon, so Beware—'

'Hello!' said a voice. 'You've been a long time. I have been waiting for hours,' and Hare saw the red-coated gentleman sitting on a stile. At the same moment a strange odour came floating to him, and a dim memory awoke of stories he had heard round the fire at a little house so far away.

His heart fluttered and bumped against his side.

'Oh! Sir!' said he, 'you quite startled me. I had forgotten about you.'

'Why, young fellow, I've been expecting you to supper,' replied the Fox with a leer.

'I'm afraid it's too late, I haven't time, thank you. I'll put off my visit, if you don't mind,' said the Hare.

'It's quite early, and really you *must* come, everything is ready, even the red-currant jelly,' and the Fox took his arm and led him down a footpath, between the bilberry clumps, deeper and darker as they scrambled over great rocks and through patches of briar.

It was no use to resist, and Hare pretended not to be afraid. The Fox talked cheerfully all the way, but kept a tight hold of Hare's arm. Perhaps there was nothing to fear after all.

'I've got a flute,' said Hare, 'I'll show it to you if you let go my arm.' He made one more effort to get away.

'Show it to me in the house,' replied the Fox, 'and then you can play on it,' and he gave Hare's arm a pinch.

They arrived at a ruined mill house beside a stream. The Fox opened the door and pushed Hare into the kitchen. It really wasn't a gentleman's house, for ragged cobwebs of curtains hung at the windows, and feathers lay piled on the floor. The room had not been dusted for years.

Fox was an untidy animal. In a corner lay a gun, a trap, several snares, a jemmy for forcing doors, and a complete burglar's outfit, including hand-cuffs.

Hare sat uneasily on the edge of stool, and Fox lay back on a broken rocking-chair.

On the table was a very large dish, as big as Hare, a plate, a long cruel knife and sharp fork, and a pot of red-currant jelly.

'Do you know anything about jugging?' asked Fox, but Hare had never heard of it, and he shook his head.

'It's a new dish, very delicious with jelly,' returned the Fox, dreamily, and he slowly licked his lips.

Hare felt more and more uncomfortable. 'I really must go,' said he, as the stars blinked at

him through the broken window, and a little wind moaned round the house. Was Grey Rabbit sitting up for him? Would the Squirrel miss him?

'Not yet, not yet. You've only just come, and I've had no company lately,' said the Fox. 'Would you mind taking off your coat and weskit? They might fit a young friend of mine.'

Hare got more and more alarmed. He handed his lovely blue coat and waistcoat to the Fox, and a paper fell out of the pocket.

'Hello, what's this?' asked the Fox, as he put Hare's watch round his neck, and opened the paper covered with noughts and crosses.

'It's a game,' stammered Hare, 'it's the things I collect.'

'Let us play,' said the Fox, and he drew his chair up to Hare's stool, so that his paws touched Hare's.

'Oh, no, I don't feel well,' faltered Hare.

'Dinner will soon put you right,' and the Fox leaned back and laughed and laughed at Hare's sad face.

So Hare taught noughts and crosses to the Fox, and each game he thought was the last he would play. Fox learned quickly and beat him every time. Hare was too frightened to look what he was doing; his eyes were glancing round the room to find a way of escape. The door was locked, and the broken window gave the only chance.

'That's enough,' said the Fox, putting the

pencil and paper in his pocket, and he picked up the coat and turned out the pockets. He brought out the silk handkerchief, and the bundle of ash twigs, a boot-lace, the little slippers, a marble, the flute, and the bottle of Venom.

'Hello? What have we here?' said he, examining the small green bottle. 'Scent? What? Scent? Conceited Hare to carry scent in your pocket!'

He took out the cork and poured some of the liquid on the silk handkerchief. Then he put it to his nose. His eyes closed, his ears drooped, and he sank with his head on the table, insensible.

Hare sprang up, seized the half-empty bottle of Venom, cut the watch from the Fox's neck with his new knife, swept up the slippers, the flute, and the ash twigs in his paw, and made for the window. He scrambled through, without waiting

for his coat and stick, for already the Fox's eyes were rolling, and his legs kicking.

Away he ran through the wood, tumbling over stones, pitching into brambles, slipping, sliding, rolling down the slopes, his breath panting, his eyes starting.

At first he had no idea where he was, but a glance at the stars showed him the way. He crossed the railway line, and ran through the edge of the village, where dim lights shone in the windows.

When he arrived at the spring he found four sleepy little Rabbits, and a Hedgehog, waiting for him.

'Here he comes, here he comes. Here is Columbus Hare. Hurrah!' they cried. 'What time is it? We've waited for ages.'

'Half-past twelve,' panted Hare, and he stopped a moment to breathe.

'You've been a long time exploring,' said the Hedgehog.

'I stopped to play noughts and crosses with Mr Fox,' said Hare, and they all opened wide their mouths with astonishment.

'I didn't forget your ashen twigs,' he continued, giving them the bundle. Then he hurried on without waiting for thanks, up the steep field to the wood.

Each little animal took his twig with the tiny black horse-shoes for luck and nailed it over his door.

'It's been wonderful to meet a real explorer,' they said.

Hare clasped the bottle of Venom tightly in his paw as he went through the deep wood, ready for any Weasel or Stoat whom he might meet, but nobody was abroad. As he ran out of the trees he saw a candle burning in the window of the little house, and he shouted for joy.

Grey Rabbit and Squirrel heard him, and came running down the garden path.

'Oh, Hare, we thought you were dead, especially as Wise Owl told us there was a Fox in Bilberry Wood,' they cried, as they clung to him.

'He caught me,' confessed Hare, 'and I only escaped through Toad's kind present to us all.' He gave a shiver as he thought of the Bilberry Wood and smiling Mr Fox. They entered the house and Hare told his story, and put his presents on the table.

Squirrel tootled on the flute, and little Grey Rabbit tried on the silver birch slippers, which fitted her as if they had been made for her small feet. The Venom she locked up in the medicine cupboard, among the stores of camomile, wormwood, and rue.

'I've had my great adventure,' said Hare. 'I am famous all over the world, and now I shall lead a quiet life at the fire-side.' He wound up his watch, took his lighted candle, and went slowly upstairs to bed.

Grey Rabbit and Squirrel looked at one another and laughed softly. Then they followed, and soon the only sounds in the house by the wood were the snores of Columbus Hare.

The Story
of Fuzzypeg
the Hedgehog

Early one summer morning, when the white mist lay over the fields like a soft blanket, old Hedgehog uncurled himself and rolled out of bed with a flop! on the floor.

'Don't wake Fuzzypeg,' called Mrs Hedgehog, warningly, as he rubbed his bruised shin, and struggled with a sheet which was all mixed up with his prickles, 'and don't tear the bedclothes.'

Hedgehog managed to get unravelled without spoiling the leaf-linen sheet of which Mrs Hedgehog was so proud. He stooped over little Fuzzypeg, who lay curled up in his bed, a small dusky ball of prickles.

'He'll be a grand fellow when he is grown up,' said he to his wife.

Over the head of the bed hung a string of coloured bobbins, a present from Little Grey Rabbit, who lived in the house on the edge of the Wood, and on the floor lay a poppy-head drum.

Hedgehog went downstairs with his prickles lowered, lest they should brush the white-wash off the ceiling, and walked into the kitchen. Mrs Hedgehog polished him up with a duster, and gave him a clean brown handkerchief.

He opened the door and took down a small wooden yoke, which hung on a low branch of a sycamore tree.

He slung it across his shoulders with the two chains hanging, one on each side. On the hooks of these he hung two little wooden pails, and, hitching them up, he started off to get the milk.

'Don't be late,' called Mrs Hedgehog, as she shut the door. 'Remember, breakfast is at six o'clock today. It is Fuzzypeg's birthday.'

The mist was so thick he could scarcely see, but he trotted down the beaten path, through the furze gate, as prickly as himself, into the fields.

The grass was ready for cutting, and Hedgehog was up to the ears in red sorrel and buttercups. Soon he was soaking wet with the heavy grass pushing against his knees.

He walked straight through the meadow, under a five-barred gate, which gave little room for his yoke and pails, to another field of short pasture grass. A low deep sound of breathing reached him, and out of the whiteness appeared a herd of cows, dozing as they stood waiting for the sunrise.

'Coo-up, coo-up,' called Hedgehog, and a roan-and-white Cow raised her head and watched him unhook his pails and remove the yoke. Hedgehog gave her a nudge. 'Lie down,' he commanded, and she obediently lay down.

'There's going to be a fine sunrise this morning,' said the Cow.

'How do you know that?' said Hedgehog, as he squatted down beside the Cow, and drew the tinkling stream of milk into the little pail.

'By the clouds, like curds and whey,' answered the Cow. 'When they are like butter, it will be dull,' she continued.

'And what happens when the clouds are like eggs?' asked Hedgehog, smacking his lips at the word 'eggs'.

'Then it will rain!' said the Cow, decidedly.

'Talking of eggs, I shouldn't mind one myself,' Hedgehog remarked.

'Plenty in the hen-house,' replied the Cow.

Hedgehog was silent for a few minutes, as he milked steadily, his mind running on eggs. The little pails were soon frothing over with milk, so he politely thanked the Cow, and took up his yoke.

Off he walked, slowly now, with brimming pails, across the meadows to the house where lived Grey Rabbit and her friends, Hare and Squirrel.

Hedgehog knocked at the door, and Grey Rabbit, in her white collar and cuffs, fresh as a daisy, opened it.

'You are early this morning, Hedgehog,' she said.

'Yes, Grey Rabbit, it is my little Fuzzypeg's birthday,' replied the Hedgehog.

'How old is he?' asked Grey Rabbit, at once excited and interested.

'A year – half-grown up,' said the Hedgehog.

'Wait a minute, and I will send him a present,' said Grey Rabbit, and she scampered upstairs to the attic, whilst Hedgehog measured out the milk.

She camed running down with a hen's egg.

'It's a Boiled Egg,' she said. 'I boiled it all day. Little Fuzzypeg can play ball with it.'

Hedgehog thanked her, and picked a cabbage leaf from the garden. He made it into a bag, and put the egg inside. Then he tied it to the milk pail.

'Where's that Boiled Egg?' he heard the voice of Hare crying. 'Grey Rabbit, I want that Boiled Egg for my breakfast.' So he hurried away before the Hare could take it back.

He walked down the garden path, along the lane, and across a big field to Mole's house. Moldy Warp lived underground, in a large castle, with many passages and rooms. The Hedgehog went to one of the back doors and knocked three times.

The door opened a crack, and a little pink hand stuck out, holding a stone milkjug.

'You are early this morning, Hedgehog,' said the Mole. 'I was in my larder arranging things on the shelves. On one I put Blue-bottles, Blue-bells, Blue-berries; on another Red Currants, Red Herrings, Red Radishes; on another Green Cabbage, Green Chutney, Green Grasshoppers; on another Black Berries....'

'I'm afraid I must go,' interrupted the Hedgehog. 'It is little Fuzzypeg's birthday today.'

'Wait a minute and I will send him a present,' said the Mole. He disappeared down the passage, and Hedgehog measured out the milk.

When he returned he carried a hen's egg.

'It's a Scrambled Egg,' said he. 'I had to scramble under a hay-stack and scramble back with it.'

'Oh, thank you, kind Moldy Warp,' said the Hedgehog, putting the scrambled egg with the boiled one in his cabbage-leaf bag. 'Fuzzypeg *will* be pleased; he always wanted a scrambled egg.'

He walked across the field, through a gap, and under a stone wall, to an old black house. He knocked at the door and a Rat answered. Hedgehog felt slightly nervous at Rat's house, and never turned his back, although Rat seemed a friendly fellow.

'Here's the milk,' said Hedgehog, quickly.

'You're in a hurry today,' said the Rat.

'Yes, it's my little Fuzzypeg's birthday.'

'And how old is he?' asked the Rat.

'A year,' said Hedgehog, feeling uneasy.

'I will send him a present,' said the Rat, who wanted to be on good terms with Hedgehog.

He ran to his cupboard and took out from among clubs, blunderbusses, traps and springs, an egg. 'It's a Poached Egg,' he said solemnly. 'I poached it last night from the hen-house.'

Hedgehog put it in his cabbage bag with the other eggs.

Thank you, Rat,' he said politely, as he walked backwards out of the yard and through the gate to the field.

There was one more house to visit, and that was Red Squirrel's, a house in the pine tree. Hedgehog knocked at the door, and Red Squirrel, who was always full of jokes, came tumbling downstairs and bumped into Hedgehog, nearly upsetting the rest of the milk.

'You are early with the milk, Hedgehog,' said he, throwing his jug into the air and catching it.

'Yes,' said the sober Hedgehog, who did not like such pranks. 'It is little Fuzzypeg's birthday and I must be quick. He is a year old today.'

'Your little Fuzzypeg's birthday? I must send him a present,' and he ran indoors, and pattered up and up the long stairs, to the top of the tree.

He came down carrying an egg, a dark-brown egg.

'It's an Old-Laid Egg,' said he, 'the same age as Fuzzypeg,' and he laughed as he gave it to Hedgehog.

So Hedgehog put the Old-Laid Egg with the others and hurried home with the remainder of the milk.

'How kind everyone is!' he thought, as he trotted rapidly across a ditch, and through gaps and gates to his house under the sycamore tree.

Fuzzypeg was sitting on a little chair, waiting for his bread and milk, and Mrs Hedgehog was making the toast when Hedgehog arrived.

'All these presents for Fuzzypeg,' said he, putting the eggs on the table, and he told them the story of each one.

Fuzzypeg had the Scrambled Egg for breakfast, and divided the Poached Egg between father and mother. The Old-Laid Egg and the Boiled Egg he kept for toys.

After breakfast, while Mrs Hedgehog washed

the little wooden pails and tidied up, Hedgehog went out with his son to play 'Rolling'. They climbed up a hill with the eggs, curled themselves into balls, and rolled down to the bottom.

'Bumpitty Bump!' went Fuzzypeg.

'Bumpitty Bump!' went old Hedgehog.

'Bumpitty Bump!' went the Boiled Egg.

'Squishitty Squash!' went the Old-Laid Egg.

Such a smell arose! All the little earwigs, caterpillars, wood-creepers, beetles, flies, and grasshoppers, who were walking about on the hill, taking the morning air, fainted, and Hedgehog and Fuzzypeg took to their heels and ran all the way home. After a time they ventured back to get the Boiled Egg, and Hedgehog vowed he would punish the bad Red Squirrel, by giving him no milk.

But Fuzzypeg said: 'It was rather funny, you

know, to see everyone stretched out. I should like an egg like that for a Weasel.'

When evening came and the sun went down in a sea of gold, Hedgehog gave Fuzzypeg his present – a green parcel.

Fuzzypeg opened it with trembling paws. Inside the wrapper was a little white cage, made of the pith of rushes, curiously woven, like a basket, with a handle. Two small black creatures lay within.

As he held the cage, twilight came, and the stars began to peep in the green sky. The little creatures sent out a beautiful soft light, so that the cage was like a fairy lantern.

'What are they?' asked Fuzzypeg, whispering in happy wonder.

'Glow-worms,' replied Hedgehog. 'Two tame glow-worms. Feed them and treat them kindly, and then you can let them loose in the hedge-garden.'

Fuzzypeg hung up the cage from a hook in the ceiling, and the room was filled with the delicate light. But when he came down the next day, the glow-worms were fast asleep, and so they remained till evening, when they shone like captive stars.

Hedgehog was very fond of eggs, and began to poach. He hunted in barns and outhouses, in hedges and woodstacks, but usually he found nothing, for Rat had been there first.

Then, on a lovely September day, he had a great adventure. He was strolling through the fields, near the farm, holding Fuzzypeg's hand, and keeping a sharp lookout for stray eggs, when suddenly the Hens began to cry and hiss and scream.

'Help! Help! Help! Save us! Run for your life!' they cried, and they rushed with wings outstretched and legs wide apart to the shelter of the farm. All except a Speckledy Hen, who was too frightened to move. She stood staring at an adder, which glided nearer and nearer.

Fuzzypeg trembled and stayed very still, but Hedgehog sprang at the adder's tail, and held it with teeth and hands. The adder whipped round and darted its tongue at Hedgehog. Fuzzypeg screamed and shut his eyes, but, equally quickly, old Hedgehog had curled himself like a furze ball, a solid mass of spears, with the end of the snake's tail inside.

Over and over again the adder tried to bite Hedgehog, only to be met by the sharp, dense prickles. Old Hedgehog never let go until the adder lay dead.

The Speckledy Hen came up, quivering and shaking.

'Hedgehog, you saved my life,' said she.

'It's nothing. Pray don't mention it,' said Hedgehog, modestly. A crowd from the farmyard hurried across to congratulate him.

'Three cheers for Hedgehog!' cried the barn-door Cock. 'Cock-a-doodle-*Doo!* Cock-a-doodle-*Doo!* Cock-a-doodle-*Doo!*'

'It's months since I tasted Adder Pie,' said Hedgehog. 'My wife will be glad of this,' and he slung the Adder across his back, and went home with the admiring Fuzzypeg.

After a fine dinner of Adder Pie, Fuzzypeg ran out to play 'Hide and Seek' in the larch wood, with his cousins, Tim and Bill Hedgehog, who lived in a cottage in the wood.

'I say, you fellows!' said he, thrusting out his quills, and holding his nose in the air, 'I say! My father killed a Nadder! He pounced on it! Yes, *pounced* on it, and held the tip-tippit of its tail till it was dead.'

'That's nothing,' said Bill Hedgehog, scornfully. 'My father pounced on a Lion's tail and held it till it was dead!'

Fuzzypeg ran in and out of the slender trees, treading on the larch needles, hiding among the ferns, pretending to enjoy himself, but his heart

94

was heavy and his quills drooped. He did not even stop to talk to a young rabbit, who peeped longingly from her door, wishing to be invited to join in the game.

'I don't want to play today,' he said at last, and he walked home through the bracken, expecting to meet a full-grown Lion, and wondering what he should do.

His mother was sewing a pair of leather shoes for him, with a gorse needle, and his father sat at the door mending a milk pail.

'Mother,' said he, 'if my father met a Lion, could he pounce on its tail and hold tight till it was dead?'

'Of course he could,' replied Mrs Hedgehog, looking up from her sewing, and old Hedgehog proudly rattled the milk pail, and wisely said nothing.

'He could fight an elephant, I expect,' said Fuzzypeg to himself, and he held up his head again.

'Tell me the tale of how Grey Rabbit killed the Weasel,' he implored his mother, and she told him the old story.

He made up his mind to be very brave like his father and Grey Rabbit.

Every morning the grateful Speckledy Hen laid an egg under the sycamore tree, and every day Mrs Hedgehog divided it neatly into three parts, for Hedgehog, Fuzzypeg and herself. She wanted to repay the kindness of the Hen, so one day she made a hay-seed cake.

'Take this to the Speckledy Hen,' she said to Fuzzypeg. 'Do not dawdle on the way home. Walk on the little green path under the hedgerow, not on the broad white road across the fields. There are dangers about – Weasels, Stoats, Snakes, and worse.'

'What shall I do if I meet a danger?' asked Fuzzypeg.

'Roll up in a ball, and keep your face hidden.'

'Suppose I meet a Lion?'

His mother laughed and gave him a ginger-bread to eat on the way. 'You won't meet a Lion,' said she.

He trotted through the fields, picking a few mushrooms and blackberries. He sniffed at the honeysuckle, far above his head, and admired the red rose-hips. When he got to the Low Meadow he met the Speckledy Hen.

'Mother sent you a hay-seed cake,' said he, 'and she thanks you for the nice eggs.'

'How deliciously sweet it smells!' said the Hen, taking the brown cake. 'Now come with me and I will show you where the finest acorns fall.'

She took him up to a great old oak tree, and he picked the young fallen acorns. Then she led him to a ditch to watch the Frogs play 'leap-frog'.

By the time he started home it was getting late. The blackbirds were calling, 'Hurry up, hurry up', to their children, and the thrush was practising her music for next day's wood-concert.

'You are late, little Hedgehog,' called a Robin, as he flew on his way with a letter in his beak.

'Stop and play a minute,' said the Hare, who sat warming his ears in the slanting rays of the setting sun.

Fuzzypeg stopped a minute, and a minute, and a minute, whilst the Hare tried to explain noughts and crosses to him.

Then he turned again for home, singing and shouting for joy in the evening.

''Ware Stoat! 'Ware Stoat!' cawed a Rook, flying to his family, and the excited cry of the Blackbird in the hedge decided him. He would go along the white path and leave the hedgerow.

He hurried along the broad easy road, thinking of his supper, and the game of noughts and crosses he would teach his father. Suddenly he saw a great, white, curly-haired animal bounding towards him, leaping in the air like a lamb.

He hesitated, and the animal saw him. It roared, and sprang towards him with frightful springs.

'A Lion,' thought poor Fuzzypeg, dropping his acorns and mushrooms. He gathered himself bravely together, and prepared to spring on its tail, but the animal had no tail, or if it had, it was as short as Grey Rabbit's.

'A Lion without a tail!' cried Fuzzypeg, and he curled himself up in a ball and kicked off his shoes.

The Lion bounced into him, and got a bunch of prickles in his nose. 'Bow-Wow! Bow-Wow! Ough! Ugh!' he cried, retreating.

Fuzzypeg peeped out between his prickles, and saw the Lion advancing again to the attack. He put his head under his arm and waited.

'Bow-Wow! Bow-Wow! Ow! Ow!! Ow!!!'

roared the Lion, with more prickles sticking into him, and he turned and ran to—Oh! Horrors! Fuzzypeg saw a great Elephant advancing, also without a tail!

'Good Dog, Spot; keep off him!' cried a voice, and Fuzzypeg was picked up, put in a large handkerchief, and carried away.

He had just made a hole, and was preparing to escape, when he was dropped with a thump.

'Look what Spot and I found, Daddy! A young Hedgehog!'

'Put it in the garden, Tommy; it will catch slugs.'

'No, I won't, I *won't* catch slugs!' squeaked Fuzzypeg. 'Let me go home. My father is a great Hedgehog, and he once killed a Lion.'

Tommy took no notice, but carried the Hedgehog to the garden, and put him on the path. Slowly Fuzzypeg uncurled and had a peep. Then he bolted for the gate, but he was not quick enough, for Tommy seized him, and put him under an enormous flower-pot. He brought him a bowl of bread and milk, and left him for the night.

When no little Hedgehog came home, old Hedgehog went out to look for him, along the green lanes and by-ways. He traced him to the field where he had met the Hare, and on the ground there he found a little paper with O's and X's. Hedgehog could not read it, so he put it in his pocket, and followed the track along the white path. A bundle of acorns tied up in a tiny dirty handkerchief lay there, some mushrooms screwed up in a dock leaf, and a pair of red shoes.

As he examined these, he felt a pair of eyes staring at him, and, turning, he saw the Stoat in the hedge.

Old Hedgehog never knew how he got home to his wife. He was in despair as he showed her the shoes and the pathetic little bundles. But Mrs Hedgehog would not give in.

'You must go this very night to Grey Rabbit's House to ask if they know anything,' she said. So Hedgehog set off again, under the golden September moon.

He knocked at the door, and Squirrel answered.

'No, we don't want any milk tonight, thank you,' said she, shutting the door.

'Please, ma'am, it's my little Fuzzypeg, he's lost.'

'Does anyone know where Fuzzypeg Hedgehog is?' she called into the house.

Grey Rabbit came running with a half-knitted sock in her paws, and Hare came with a little green book he was reading.

'I've seen him,' said Hare. 'We met in the Low Meadow, and we had a little game of noughts and crosses. He will be quite good at it when he grows up, if he practises.'

Hedgehog took the paper from his pocket.

'Yes, that's it, the very paper,' said Hare.

'What happened then?' asked Hedgehog.

'He just ran on and on, and I ran the other way.'

Grey Rabbit then spoke. 'I am sorry, Hedgehog. I advise you to see Wise Owl.'

'Wise Owl? Oh no, not Wise Owl!' cried Hedgehog.

'Why not?'

'Because,' and here Hedgehog hesitated, embarrassed, 'because he might be hungry, you see.'

'If you wave a white handkerchief for a truce, you will be safe,' said Squirrel, quickly, as if she did it every day.

'Can you lend me one, or even two?' asked Hedgehog. 'We only use brown ones at our house.'

Little Grey Rabbit tied two white handkerchiefs to his prickles, and he went into the great Wood.

Wise Owl was out hunting when Hedgehog rang the silvery bell, which hung on the door of the old oak tree. So he sat down to wait, feeling very small and lonely. High up among the pointed leaves he could see the kindly Moon, which had run with him through the Wood, and away, caught among the fountain leaves of a silver birch, was a cluster of twinkly little stars, 'like a Hedgehog in the sky', he thought. He crept closer to the tree and held his nose against the rough warm bark. It was comforting.

'Too whit, too whoo,' came nearer and nearer, and Wise Owl, who had heard the bell far away, flew to his house, carrying something which Hedgehog preferred not to see.

'Who are you?' he asked the little creature down below.

'Please, Sir, I'm Hedgehog the Milkman.'

'What do you want?'

'Please, Sir, I've lost my little Hedgehog, and Grey Rabbit thought you could find him for me.'

The Owl was flattered and shook his feathers.

'Perhaps I can,' he replied proudly, 'but I must be paid.'

'Anything you like,' said the Hedgehog.

'Well,' said Wise Owl, considering, as he stroked his beak, 'I will have a quill for a pen and a can of milk, and a new-laid egg. Bring them tomorrow at dawn, and you shall have news of your son.'

Hedgehog thanked him and went home, keeping a wary eye for Stoats, Weasels, and Badgers on the way.

Wise Owl flew with wide sweeping wings over the fields that night looking for little Hedgehog, but nowhere could he see him.

'Stoat, have you seen little Hedgehog?' he asked a shifty-eyed light-haired fellow, creeping along the hedges with a club in his hand.

'No, Sir,' said Stoat. 'I only saw Milkman Hedgehog a moment.'

'If you see him, report to me,' said Wise Owl, sternly.

'Yes, Sir,' said Stoat, touching his slouched hat, and grinning a crooked grin. 'I wish I had seen him,' he muttered when Wise Owl had flown away.

'Rat, have you seen little Hedgehog?' the Owl asked a dark poacher, creeping under a wall with a twisty wire in his hand.

'No, Sir. I sent him an egg for his birthday, but I've not seen him.'

'Report to me if you do,' said Wise Owl.

'Yes, Sir,' said the Rat, touching his cap, and hurrying on.

'Yard-dog, have you seen little Hedgehog?' the Owl asked a curly white dog, sitting outside his kennel, singing to the Moon.

'Yes,' answered the dog. 'I've seen him, but I shall tell you nothing about him. I belong to the House, and you belong to the Wood,' and the dog proudly shook his chain and continued his song.

'He must be somewhere near,' thought the Owl, so he searched the lawn and pigsty, the drying-ground and orchard.

A little sound caught his keen ears, as he flew slowly over the garden, a sound of weeping and soft sobbing.

'Mother, Mother, Grey Rabbit, Father, Moldy Warp. Come! Come! Oh! I'm so lonely and lost!'

The sounds came from a large inverted flower-pot, standing firmly in the rhubarb bed. The Owl flew down and looked through the hole in the top.

The sobbing ceased, for little Fuzzypeg was terribly alarmed to see a bright eye instead of the far cluster of stars.

'Is that you, little Hedgehog?' asked the Owl.

'Yes, it's me,' said the little creature, trembling.

'Help is coming,' said the Owl, and he flew away home, for his work was over.

At dawn came the Hedgehog through the great Wood, carrying a can of milk, a goose-quill for a pen, and a new-laid egg. He rang the bell and waved the handkerchiefs. Owl, who was just getting ready for bed, looked through the door.

'Put them down there, Hedgehog. Your son is safe under a flower-pot in the Farmer's garden.'

Hedgehog thanked him and started home at a run, calling on his way for Little Grey Rabbit, Hare, Squirrel, and Moldy Warp. Mrs Hedgehog ran to the door when she heard the patter of little feet, and she joined them. They all ran through the fields, Hare and Little Grey Rabbit leading, Squirrel coming next...

Hedgehog and Mrs Hedgehog panting after . . .

. . . and Moldy Warp far behind.

They squeezed under the gate (except the fat Hare, who had to climb the wall), and ran across the lettuces and carrots, down the little path between the gooseberry bushes, to the red rhubarb, where stood an enormous plant-pot.

'Are you there, Fuzzypeg?' called old Hedgehog.

'Yes, Father, are you?' answered a small faint voice.

'Yes, we are all here,' said Hedgehog, 'Squirrel, Hare and Grey Rabbit, and Moldy Warp is on the way.'

He turned to the animals. 'All push, and over the plant-pot must go.'

So they pushed and they pushed, but the plant-pot didn't move, and they pushed and they shoved, and the plant-pot *still* did not move.

'Steady, boys! Now! All together! Shove!!' called Hedgehog, but still the plant-pot did not move.

A large Rat strolled up. 'What are you people doing?' said he.

'Little Hedgehog is under this plant-pot,' explained Hedgehog, raising his prickles.

'Oh, he's found, is he? Wise Owl asked me to keep a lookout for him. But you will never move that thing if Hare pushes one way and you all push the other.'

Hare blushed and went over to Grey Rabbit.

'Now, heave Ho!!!' shouted Rat, but as they all pushed away from him, the plant-pot still did not move.

They stuck their little feet in the ground, and puffed and panted and bumped their shoulders, and got pricked by Hedgehog, and kicked by Hare, and frightened by Rat. Little Hedgehog inside shouted, 'Push harder! Push harder!'

They rested a moment, and wiped their hot brows with the two handkerchiefs on Hedgehog's prickles.

Then Moldy Warp turned up.

'Not that way,' said he, quietly. 'If the pot fell over, you would all be squashed. This is the way.'

He planted his feet firmly, and with nose and hands dug rapidly into the soil by the flower-pot. Earth flew in a shower, and in a few seconds he disappeared down the tunnel he had made. The animals waited, breathless.

Fuzzypeg crawled up the tunnel, to be hugged, prickles and all, by Old Hedgehog and his wife. A minute later came Mole, wiping his lips.

'I stopped to finish his bread and milk,' he explained. 'It was a pity to waste it.'

He rammed the soil down in the tunnel, and the happy procession started home.

'Don't forget to tell Wise Owl that I found little Hedgehog,' called the Rat as he ran off.

'Come into the garden and have some refreshments,' said Mrs Hedgehog, when they got back. So they all sat under the sycamore tree, whilst she spread a cloth on the grass.

Then Hedgehog and Mrs Hedgehog brought egg sandwiches, acorns baked in their skins, rose-hip jam, fresh blackberries and cream, mushrooms on toast, and crab-apple cider.

When the Hare, the Squirrel, and the Little Grey Rabbit went home, they each took a small quill pen, which the grateful Hedgehog had made for them; but Moldy Warp wouldn't have anything, for, he said, digging was more in his line than writing, and he had everything he wanted in his castle under the Ten-Acre field.

Patricia Cleveland-Peck
The String Family 90p

The miniature world of the String family – Mr and Mrs String, their
children, Hemp, Flax, Twine and baby Skein all come alive and share their
adventures with Sally in Miss Floribunda's cottage in the country. Sally is
the only human child to be introduced to the String family and friends – a
wonderland of aunts and cousins with exciting and exotic names – the
Binder Twines, the Garden Lines and the Embroidery Silks.

Walt Disney
Adventures of Mickey Mouse £1.25

Meet Mickey Mouse – with his friends Henry Horse, Carolyn Cow,
Patricia Pig, Clara Cluck the Hen and Robert Rooster, best friends all of
them ... except Hound Dog, who does seem to be on the grumpy side,
and Claws the Cat, who likes to sit for hours ready to pounce outside
Mickey's front door – which is actually his mouse hole.

With such a collection of friends we can expect lots of adventures from
the most famous mouse of the century.

Ann Lawrence
Oggy at Home 70p

Oggy the hedgehog has come a long, long way since the days when he
thought Hampstead Heath was the whole world ... When Oggy is woken
up from his long winter sleep, having moved to the countryside, a silly
kitten tells him she's 'only exploring' his new home – and Oggy is not
very pleased: a well travelled hedgehog deserves more respect, he
thinks, and he sets about teaching Tiggy the scatter-brained kitten a thing
or two about the wide, wide world.

chosen by Christopher Logue
The Children's Book of Comic Verse 95p

Nothing to do? Nothing to do?
Put some mustard in your shoe,
Fill your pockets full of soot,
Drive a nail into your foot,
Put some sugar in your hair,
And your toys upon the stair . . .

– or laugh, scream and be ill with this super collection of the best comic
verse.

Patrick Dowling
The Amazing Adventures of Morph:
Birthday Party 90p

Morph, a BBC television star, and his friend, Tony Hart, tell us of the
adventures of his happy, but sometimes naughty, 'under the table'
family: Gran Morph, the skateboarder; Chas, the faithful hound; Delilah
and Folly, the ladies in the group; and Gillespie, who thinks a lot!

You can buy these and other Piccolo books from booksellers and
newsagents; or direct from the following address:
Pan Books, Sales Office, Cavaye Place, London SW10 9PG
Send purchase price plus 35p for the first book and 15p for
each additional book, to allow for postage and packing
Prices quoted are applicable in the UK

While every effort is made to keep prices low, it is sometimes
necessary to increase prices at short notice. Pan Books reserve
the right to show on covers and charge new retail prices which
may differ from those advertised in the text or elsewhere